The Missing Cat

by Susan McCloskey
illustrated by Jane Dippold

Meg   Hugs

"Come on, Hugs," Meg said. "It's time for your dinner." She gave Hugs some cat food. Hugs sniffed at the food. Then he turned his head away.

"You don't want that food, do you, Hugs?" Meg said. "Do you want chicken today?"

Meg gave Hugs a new can of cat food. But he still did not eat.

"Hugs won't eat!" Meg said to Gram. "He won't eat the chicken or beef. He doesn't want the turkey or the turkey with cheese. He won't even eat the tuna!"

"I can see that," said Gram.

"But Hugs **loves** to eat," said Meg. "He never leaves a bit of food in his dish."

"He must feel sick," said Gram.

"Oh, no! Poor Hugs!" said Meg. "Will he be okay?"

"Let's call Dr. Jan, the vet," said
Gram. "She will know what to do."
Gram went to call the vet.
Meg went with Gram.

Then they came back
to the kitchen to get Hugs
and take him to the vet.
But Hugs was gone.

"Gramps, have you seen Hugs?" Meg asked.

"Let me think," said Gramps. "I read the paper, and he sat on my lap. Then I took the meatballs out of the freezer to thaw, and he watched me. But I haven't seen him since then."

"Hugs! Come here, Hugs!" Meg called. But Hugs did not come to her.

"I'll look in the closets," said Gram.

"I'll look under the beds,"
said Meg.

"I'll help you look," said Gramps.
They looked under all the tables
and behind all the curtains. They
even looked in the basement.

But they didn't find Hugs.

"Where **is** that cat?" said Meg.
"I just don't know," said Gram.
"Maybe he knows you called
Dr. Jan," said Gramps. "He doesn't
like to go to the vet. He may hide
from us for hours!"

Gramps went to put the meatballs in the oven. Meg wanted to look around the house one more time.

Soon Meg called, "Gram! Gramps! I found him! I found Hugs!"

Then Gramps called out, "I found something, too!"

"Where was Hugs?" Gram asked.

"He was in the bathroom, asleep in the tub!" Meg said. "What a silly cat!"

"And what did you find, Gramps?" Gram asked.

"I know why Hugs did not eat!" said Gramps. "And I don't think he has to go to the vet. Just look at what I found!"

"Oh, Hugs," said Meg. **"That's** why you're not hungry!"

"Hugs!" said Gram. "You ate all our meatballs!"